MW00805104

A Straw Full of Milk

Little Stinker Series
Book 5

Dave Sargent was born and raised on a dairy farm in northwest Arkansas. When he began writing in 1990, he made a decision to dedicate the remainder of his life to encouraging children to read and write. He is very good with students and teachers alike. He and his wife Pat travel across the United States together. They write about animals with character traits. They are good at showing how animals act a lot like kids.

A Straw Full of Milk

Little Stinker Series
Book 5

By Dave Sargent

Illustrated by Elaine Woodward

Ozark Publishing, Inc.
P.O. Box 228
Prairie Grove, AR 72753

Cataloging-in-Publication Data

Sargent, Dave, 1941–
   A straw full of milk / by Dave Sargent ;
illustrated by Elaine Woodward. —Prairie
Grove, AR : Ozark Publishing, c2007.
      p. cm. (Little stinker series ; 5)

   "Solve problems"—Cover.
   SUMMARY: After Dave digs a tunnel in
the hay and hides the baby skunks, he faces
another problem. When he tries to feed them
warm milk, he realizes that they don't know
how to drink.
      ISBN 1-59381-285-X (hc)
             1-59381-286-8 (pbk)

      1. Skunks—Juvenile fiction.
   2. Dogs—Juvenile fiction.
   [1. Games—Fiction.]
   I. Woodward, Elaine, 1956– ill.
   II. Title. III. Series.

      PZ7.S243St 2007
      [Fic]—dc21   2005906110

Printed in the United States of America

iv

Inspired by

the little skunks I had to feed with a straw because they were babies and didn't know how to drink milk.

Dedicated to

all my friends who love warm milk.

Foreword

After Dave digs a tunnel in the hay and hides the baby skunks, he faces another problem. When he tries to feed them warm milk, he realizes that they don't know how to drink.

Contents

If you'd like to have Dave Sargent, the author of the Little Stinker Series, visit your school free of charge, call: 1-800-321-5671.

One

Milk from Rose

I was up bright and early the next morning. Mom had breakfast ready. She had fixed biscuits, gravy, sausage and eggs. I managed to slip an extra biscuit inside my shirt while I was eating.

I also got a big piece of sausage. I had to feed Tippy. He sure loved biscuits. He loved gravy, too, but I couldn't slip any of that out.

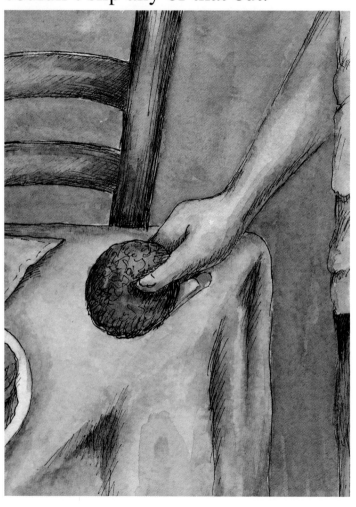

I put on my coat and headed out the door. It was still dark so I went back inside and got a lantern. My brothers and I always put out the hay. I had to make sure I got to the barn first, so I could put it out myself.

I didn't want my brothers to find the skunks. I knew it would tickle them to death if I put out all the hay. They wouldn't have any work to do. I got the hay put out by the time Dad got the cows in the corral.

When Dad started milking, I got my cup and squirted some milk from Ole Rose. Rose was the most gentle of all the cows. Anyone could milk her, anywhere. I noticed that Dad was watching me, so I turned the cup up and drank the warm milk.

Then, when he looked away, I squirted a few more squirts in my cup and gave it to Tippy. Boy, Ole Tippy loved warm milk. After a few more squirts for Tippy, I got some milk for the skunks. I hurried to the barn and pulled all the little skunks out of the den. I tried feeding them the milk.

Two

Straws Full of Milk

The little skunks didn't know how to drink yet. I'd have to teach them to drink milk, just like I had to teach baby calves to drink milk.

First, I took the little guys, one at a time, and stuck their noses in the milk. I then set them down. They licked the milk off of their faces. Then they started searching for more. They knew where the milk was. They could smell it. They just didn't know how to drink it.

After dipping their noses in the milk several times, all but three began drinking. I was running out of time. I found a piece of grass stem in the hay. It was hollow inside. I made a straw out of it. I sucked milk up in the straw. Then I squeezed the top of it and let milk dribble onto the little skunks' lips. They lapped it up.

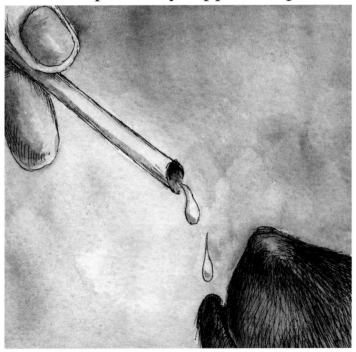

Soon, all the little fellers were full and happy. I put them back in their den and got ready for school.

I was so excited and anxious to get back home, I couldn't do much of anything all day.

When I jumped off the bus that afternoon, I was halfway from the bus stop to the house when I saw Tippy coming to meet me.

We hurried home. I changed my clothes and then ran to the barn with Tippy by my side. Tippy wanted me to play, but I wanted to play with my little skunks. I knew I'd have to share my affection with Tippy, or he'd feel bad. I didn't want that.

I played with Tippy for a few minutes. We played tug-of-war. And then we wrestled for a while.

Three

The Skunks Accept Tippy

I reached into the little skunks' den and pulled them out. Tippy backed way back. He still didn't want anything to do with the skunks. They were jumping, nibbling and sucking on my fingers and hands.

The little skunks were hungry. I told them that I'd have their supper ready in just a little while. And then I noticed Tippy inching closer and closer to the little skunks. It wasn't long until he was right beside them.

And then, the funniest thing happened. One of the little skunks climbed on Tippy's back. Tippy rolled over onto his side and froze. It was like he was afraid to move. I knew he wouldn't hurt the skunks, because he knew I liked them.

All of the little skunks ended up on top of Tippy. Tippy was black and white like they were. I think they thought that he was just a big skunk. I think that's why they liked him.

I heard Dad calling the cows. It was chore time. I gathered up all the little skunks and put them back in their den.

I put out the hay for the cows. I gathered the eggs. Then I gave the chickens some scratch. I slopped the hogs.

Now all that I had left to do was feed my skunks again. I got my tin cup and filled it half full of Rose's milk. I took the cup of milk in the barn and fed the little skunks. This time, I was able to get all of them to drink it. It took a while, but they all drank. In all, they drank about a fourth of a cup of milk. I gave Tippy the rest of the milk. I milked another half cup from Rose. I drank half of it and gave Tippy the other half.

Four

Skunk Facts

In the fall skunks eat a lot and grow a thick coat. The mothers and kits move into large dens and snuggle together to keep warm. During the winter skunks sleep. They live off of stored body fat. They are not true hibernators. They wake up often and may leave the den to search for food.